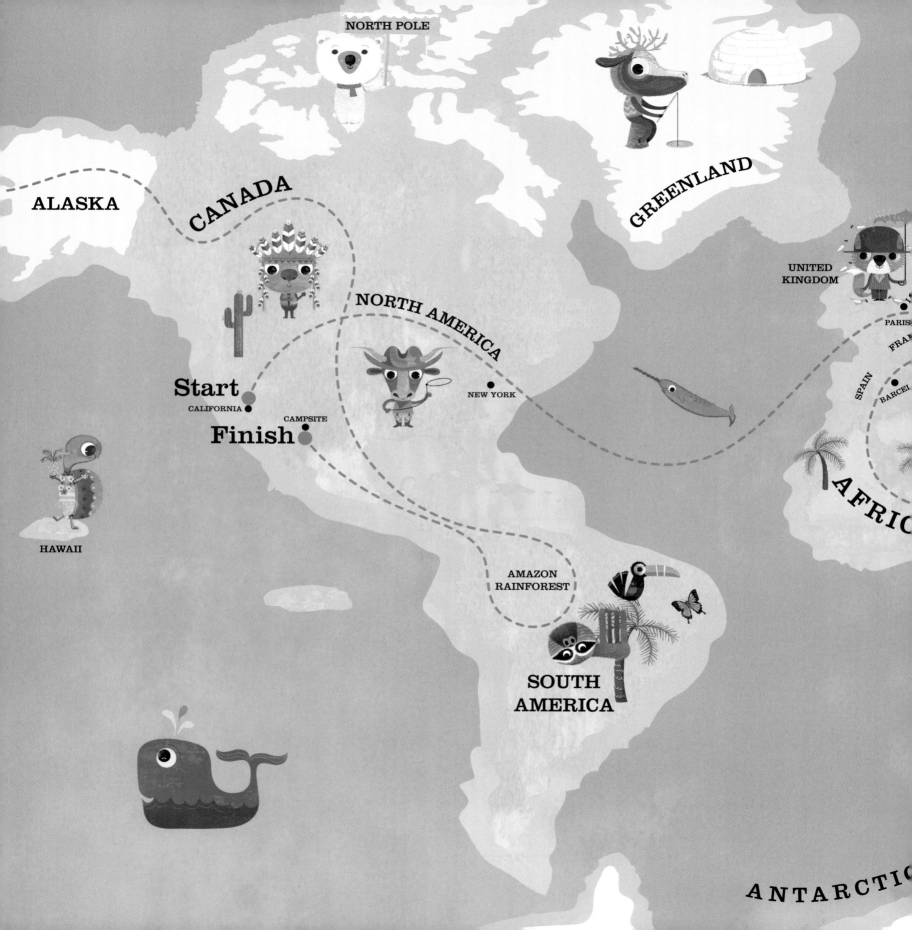

NORTH POLE

GREENLAND

ALASKA

CANADA

UNITED
KINGDOM

NORTH AMERICA

PARIS

FRAN

Start

SPAIN

CALIFORNIA

BARCEL

NEW YORK

AFRIC

Finish

CAMPSITE

HAWAII

AMAZON
RAINFOREST

SOUTH
AMERICA

ANTARCTI

IMAGINE THAT™

Licensed exclusively to Imagine That Publishing Ltd
Tide Mill Way, Woodbridge, Suffolk, IP12 1AP, UK
www.imaginethat.com
Copyright © 2019 Imagine That Group Ltd
All rights reserved
2 4 6 8 9 7 5 3 1
Manufactured in China

Written by Oakley Graham
Illustrated by Olive May Green

ISBN 978-1-78958-199-7

A catalogue record for this book is available from the British Library

Near and Far

Written by
Oakley Graham

Illustrated by
Olive May Green

Panda, **Fox** and **Donkey** are the very best of friends! They live in a place called **California**, in **North America**.

One day, the friends decided to go on a camping trip. The campsite was near their home, so they packed up their camper van and set off on the short journey.

They were so excited that they forgot where they had put the map and were soon completely …

... lost!

Panda, Fox and Donkey drove all through the day and all through the night, and for five more days after that … until they were far away in a busy city with enormous skyscrapers. They had driven all the way to **New York City!**

That evening they watched a music show on
Broadway and ate yummy hot dogs in Times Square.

The next day, the three friends reached a port. Unable to go any further, they drove the camper van on to a gigantic boat which sailed across the Atlantic Ocean to **Europe**.

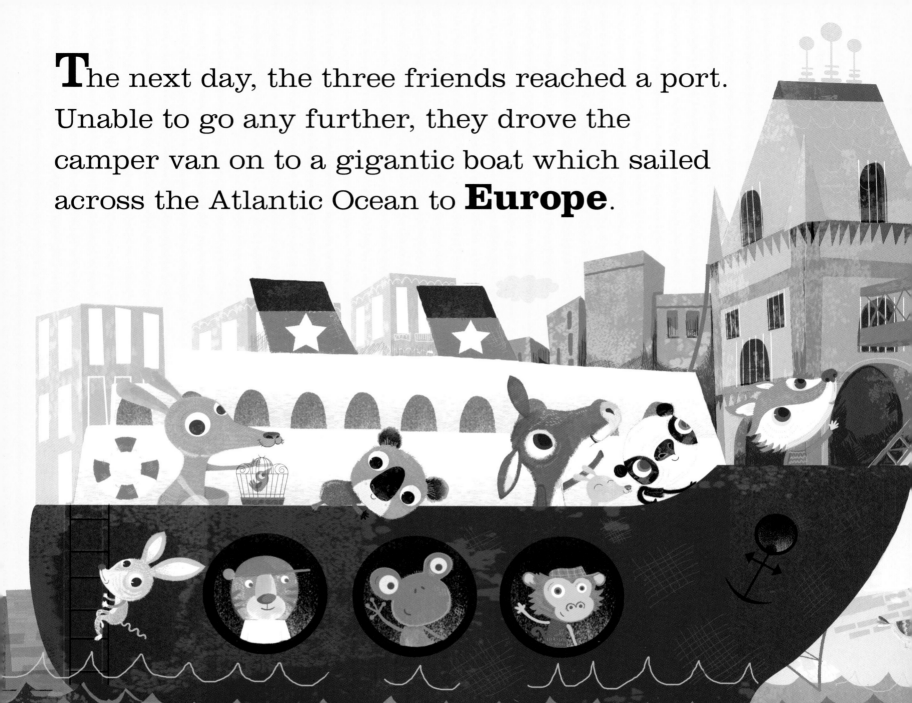

The boat took them all the way to **England!** Panda, Fox and Donkey decided that it would be rude if they didn't visit the queen in **London**.

So that's exactly what they did!

After a cup of tea with the Queen,
Donkey was feeling very hungry indeed.
'Let's go to **France!**' he suggested.
'French food is magnifique!'

Panda and Fox agreed, so they drove the
camper van on to a train. The train travelled
through a tunnel under the sea to France, and
in no time at all, the friends arrived in **Paris**.
Paris was beautiful and the food was delicious!

Once the friends were full of lovely French food, they set off again.

After a long drive, they arrived at a city called **Venice**, in **Italy**. Venice appeared to float on water! Instead of roads, it had canals, and instead of cars, everyone used boats to get around.

That evening, Panda, Fox and Donkey
travelled in a gondola to a fancy-dress ball.

It was lots of fun being lost!

The next day, the three friends travelled west, driving along beautiful coastlines until they reached a city called **Barcelona**, in **Spain**.

The buildings in Barcelona were amazing and some of the churches were incredible!

The friends needed help to find their campsite, so Fox asked a friendly swallow for directions. The bird told them to head south, so the friends followed his advice.

After a sea crossing and a lot more driving, Panda, Fox and Donkey travelled through bustling markets and past enormous pyramids, but their campsite was nowhere to be seen ... they were in **Africa!**

There were lots of amazing things to see in Africa, but the friends liked going on safari in **Kenya** the best.

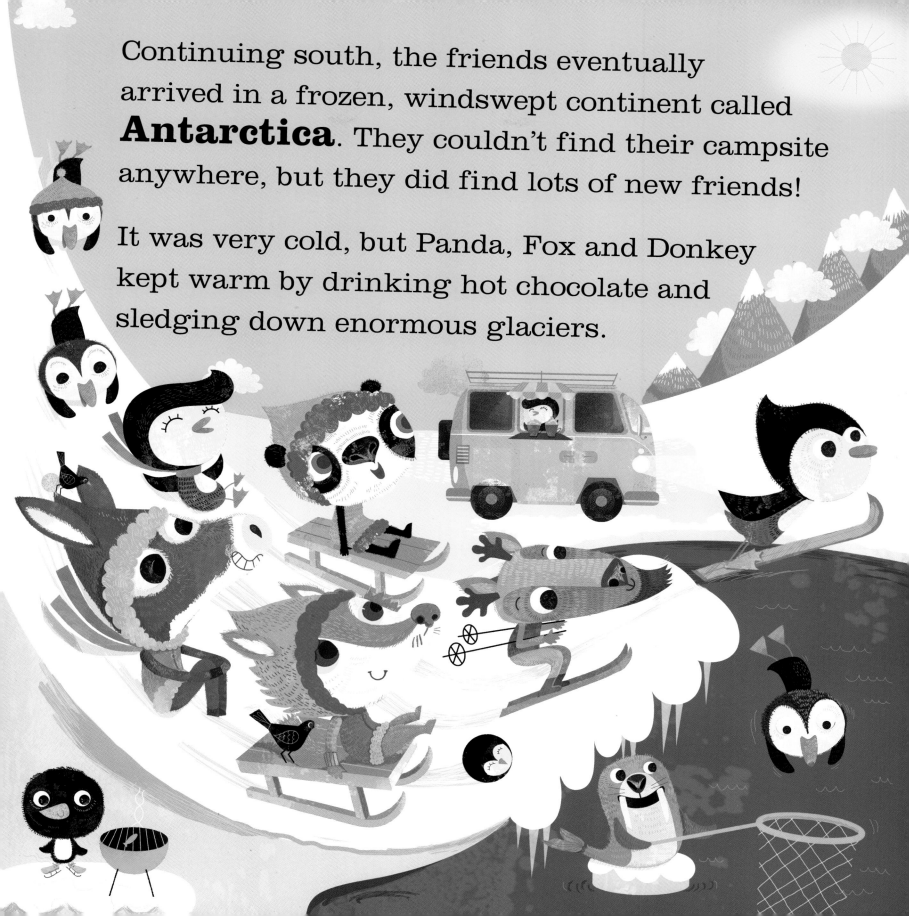

Continuing south, the friends eventually arrived in a frozen, windswept continent called **Antarctica**. They couldn't find their campsite anywhere, but they did find lots of new friends!

It was very cold, but Panda, Fox and Donkey kept warm by drinking hot chocolate and sledging down enormous glaciers.

It was too cold to stay in Antarctica, so the friends took a ship to a place called **Australia**.

Australia was amazing! The friends snorkelled at the Great Barrier Reef …

… looked at some amazing cave paintings in wild regions called 'the outback' …

... and had barbecues with new friends on the beach.

Still determined to find their campsite, the friends island-hopped all the way to **India**, in **Asia**.

There were lots of beautiful temples in India and the people were very friendly indeed.

When it was time to set off on their journey once more, Donkey really didn't want to go – he loved eating curry!

Travelling through humid swamps and jungles, the camper van soon reached **China**.

Panda stopped to say hello to some of her family, and Fox and Donkey had great fun playing with dragon kites.

But no one knew where their campsite was!

From China, the friends drove to **Russia**.
The friends loved **Moscow** and Panda especially
liked Russian dancing.

Then the friends travelled east ... it was
their longest drive yet! They saw packs of
wolves in the forests and a majestic tiger.
When they reached the Bering Sea they
made the icy crossing to **Canada**.

The campsite was quite close now, but without their map, Panda, Fox and Donkey drove straight past it!

When they reached the Amazon rainforest, in **South America**, they realised that they must have driven too far!

The friends stopped to explore and saw some amazing Amazonian animals. Then, as Fox climbed a tree to look at a particularly colourful parrot, Donkey noticed something sticking out of his jumper. It was the map!

Finding the campsite was easy with the map! Fox made a fire and the three friends toasted marshmallows and talked about all of the fun places they had visited.

From that day on, the three friends continued to travel both near and far away from home. During their travels they met lots of new people, discovered new places and learnt lots of amazing things.

NORTH POLE

GREENLAND

ALASKA

CANADA

UNITED
KINGDOM

PARIS

NORTH AMERICA

FRAN

SPAIN

BARCEL

Start

CALIFORNIA

NEW YORK

Finish

CAMPSITE

AFRIC

HAWAII

AMAZON
RAINFOREST

SOUTH
AMERICA

ANTARCTI

NDINAVIA

MOSCOW

RUSSIA

OPE

INDIA

CHINA

JAPAN

EGYPT

KENYA

MADAGASCAR

AUSTRALIA

NEW ZEALAND

SOUTH POLE

With love from
Panda, Fox and Donkey xxx

Where will they go next?